JAN 0 4

DATE DUE

5-24			
GAYLORD			PRINTED IN U.S.A.

Copyright © 2003 by Nord-Süd Verlag AG,
Gossau Zürich, Switzerland
First published in Switzerland under the title *Sandmännchens Mondfahrt*.
English translation copyright © 2003 by North-South Books Inc., New York

First published in the United States, Great Britain, Canada,
Australia, and New Zealand in 2003 by North-South Books,
an imprint of Nord-Süd Verlag AG, Gossau Zürich, Switzerland.

Distributed in the United States by North-South Books Inc., New York.

Library of Congress Cataloging-in-Publication Data is available.
A CIP catalogue record for this book is available from The British Library.
ISBN 0-7358-1789-8 (trade edition)
1 3 5 7 9 HC 10 8 6 4 2
ISBN 0-7358-1790-1 (library edition)
1 3 5 7 9 LE 10 8 6 4 2
Printed in Belgium

For more information about our books, and the authors and artists
who create them, visit our web site: www.northsouth.com

The Sandman

BY Udo Weigelt

ILLUSTRATED BY Sibylle Heusser

Translated by J. Alison James

North-South Books

NEW YORK / LONDON

Every night when the Sandman came home from dusting the eyes of people with sleep, he would make himself a cup of tea, sit in his big chair, and read. Sometimes he looked out through the clouds and watched the sun come up. When the sunlight crossed his room, he put his things away and went to bed.

But one night the Sandman realized that something was missing. He stared out the window and pondered for a while.

"That's it!" he said, and stood up. "I'm lonely. I need a friend." He decided to go and get one the very next night.

The Sandman was excited when he got into his airship the next night. As he sprinkled his sleeping sand he looked for anyone he might have missed, someone who was still awake. He found a boy and a girl!

The boy was in bed, but he was still wide awake.

"Hello!" cried the boy, astonished. "You must be the Sandman!"

"Exactly right," said the Sandman. "Would you like to be my friend?"

"Oh, yes!" cried the boy. He gave a huge yawn. "I've never been friends with a Sandman before."

"Wonderful!" said the Sandman. "We can go sailing in my airship."

"Great . . ." began the boy, and he fell fast asleep.

"You're an odd friend," said the Sandman, baffled. "Why
do you go to sleep just when I've come to visit?" He shook his
head. "Perhaps I'll have more luck with the girl."

The Sandman flew off. But in the girl's room, the *very* same
thing happened: she was excited to see the Sandman, but in the
blink of an eye, she too was sound asleep.

Disappointed, the Sandman climbed back into his airship and flew once more around the city looking for someone else who was still awake. Soon he saw a man wearing a black mask, with a sack on his back. Quickly the Sandman flew down.

"Hello," he cried. "I am the Sandman. Who are you?"

The man jumped back in surprise. "Me?" he asked. "Well, I am a . . . um, a—," he had a good yawn, "—well, to tell the truth, I'm a thief, but I think I'm much too tired tonight to . . ."

And he fell asleep, right there on the street.

The Sandman was startled. A thief! He had better find
a policeman!

The policeman that came back with the Sandman was
so terribly tired he could hardly stand up. When he found
the thief, the policeman sat down next to him—and he too
fell fast asleep!

"Why is it so hard to find a friend," the Sandman
wondered sadly.

He sat miserably at his window pondering the problem.
"That's it," he said. "People are supposed to sleep at night. I
need to make friends with an animal. A nocturnal animal!"
He decided to do so the very next night.

The next night the Sandman flew into the woods. He found many nocturnal animals: bats, foxes, and owls. They had slept all day long, so they were wide awake when the Sandman arrived. He told them who he was. He said that he was looking for a friend. Then he explained what had happened when he tried to talk to people. When he had finished, he looked around. All the animals were asleep, sound asleep.

The Sandman wanted to cry. It just wasn't fair that everybody went to sleep as soon as they saw him. "I want a friend," he said, "a friend who is awake!"

"How do people stay awake," the Sandman wondered. "That's it!" he said. "They splash water in their faces. I can visit the animals in the ocean. They have water in their faces all the time." The sea was no trouble to the Sandman. He flew right under the waves with his ship.

Deep down in the water, the Sandman
met a dolphin. He met a shark, an octopus,
and even a whale. He tried to talk with
them, but they all just smiled and fell asleep.
The Sandman wept as he rose to the
surface, and his tears mixed with the sea.

The Sandman sat on the shore. He was terribly sad. "I was so sure," he said. "I really felt that there was a friend for me. And now that I've imagined it, I can't bear to be without one."

The moon was reflected in the water. The water rippled, and the moon winked at the Sandman. *Was* it a wink? Or was it just a ripple? The Sandman looked up in the sky. The moon smiled happily down at the Sandman.

"Could that be it?" the Sandman wondered. "The moon is a long way off—but why not? I have an airship after all."

When the Sandman reached the moon, she cried out with delight, "There you are at last! I've been waiting for you to notice me."

"Were you really winking at me?" the Sandman asked.

"Of course," said the moon. "I couldn't come down to you. I couldn't even call out. I really wanted you to be my friend, but you had to notice me first."

"Oh!" cried the Sandman. "That's what I want too, a friend!" Cautiously he asked, "Won't you get sleepy if I'm around?"

"Sleepy?" The moon roared with laughter.
"Of course not. The moon is never sleepy.
Especially not when a friend has come to visit!"
    From that night on, when the Sandman was
finished sprinkling his sleeping sand, he flew up
to spend the day with his good friend, the moon.